Charles H. Pierce, W. [from old catalog] M.

The river and the sound

An account of a steamboat excursion by a party of ladies and gentlemen from

Worcester, Mass., in the summer of 1869

Charles H. Pierce, W. [from old catalog] M.

The river and the sound
An account of a steamboat excursion by a party of ladies and gentlemen from Worcester, Mass., in the summer of 1869

ISBN/EAN: 9783743467187

Manufactured in Europe, USA, Canada, Australia, Japa

Cover: Foto ©Andreas Hilbeck / pixelio.de

Manufactured and distributed by brebook publishing software (www.brebook.com)

Charles H. Pierce, W. [from old catalog] M.

The river and the sound

The River

---◆---

1869.

---◆---

And the Sound.

The River and The Sound.

Alfred S. Roe.

AN ACCOUNT OF A

STEAMBOAT EXCURSION

BY A

PARTY OF LADIES AND GENTLEMEN

FROM WORCESTER, MASS.,

IN THE SUMMER OF 1869.

WORCESTER:
PRINTED BY CHAS. HAMILTON.
PALLADIUM OFFICE.

THE COMMITTEE,

IN BEHALF OF THE

"COIT EXCURSIONISTS," OF 1869,

RESPECTFULLY

DEDICATE THIS LITTLE VOLUME TO THE

CHAPLAIN OF THE PARTY,

REV. G. J. SANGÉR.

PREFACE.

E owe no apology to our friends the "COITS" or the chance reader for presenting this little volume, as we were elected to do it. If we have succeeded in selecting and arranging such matter as faithfully gives an account of the delightful trip of 1869, and if the work in other respects meets your kind approbation, we shall be satisfied. We believe it to be the duty of every one to break loose occasionally from the restraint of business or the dull routine of domestic cares, and seek that recreation we all need, amid new scenes and under new circumstances; and we know of no trip better adapted to invigorate us physically and mentally, and inspire us with love and gratitude to the Creator of all things, than a trip upon the deep, blue sea!

> "Roll on, thou deep and dark blue ocean, roll!
> *   *   *   *   *   *   *   *   *   *   *
> Time writes no wrinkle on thine azure brow,—
> Such as creation's dawn beheld thee thou rollest now."

God never intended we should spend our days constantly engrossed with the cares of life! If he had, he would not have created a world filled with so much to enjoy and given us such capabilities for enjoying it. As much of our enjoy-

1*

ment in life depends upon the memories of the past, we hope this little record of a very pleasant excursion will serve to keep memory's links bright, and perhaps cast a pleasant beam upon some dark hour of life.

With these thoughts, kind friends, we submit the following pages to your charitable criticism, and trust we may meet many times ere we are called upon

> ———" to join
> The innumerable caravan which moves
> To that mysterious realm where each shall take
> His chamber in the silent halls of death,"

and that we may all so live as to

> ———" approach the grave
> Like one who wraps the drapery of his couch
> About him, and lies down to pleasant dreams,"

is the earnest wish of

YOUR COMMITTEE.

OFFICERS OF STEAMER.

CAPTAIN:
W. R. BROWN, New London.

FIRST PILOT:
GEORGE GEER, New London.

CHIEF ENGINEER:
FRANK BIDWELL, Norwich.

SECOND ENGINEER:
HENRY DURFEE, Norwich.

STEWARD:
JAMES LAWLESS, New London.

CHIEF MATE:
ALBERT LESTER, Lyme.

SECOND MATE:
CHARLES LESTER, Lyme.

OFFICERS OF THE PARTY.

PRESIDENT:

GEORGE R. PECKHAM.

VICE PRESIDENTS:

G. A. BARNARD,
WM. C. BARBOUR.

SECRETARY:

WM. MECORNEY.

TREASURER:

GEO. W. WHEELER.

STEWARD:

HENRY GLAZIER,

CHAPLAIN:

REV. G. J. SANGER.

NAMES OF THE PARTY.

E. E. ABBOTT,	Worcester.
Mrs. AUGUSTA ABBOTT,	"
H. H. ADAMS,	Templeton.
Mrs. H. H. ADAMS,	"
FRANK A. ATHERTON,	Worcester.
JOHN M. ALDRICH,	"
Mrs. JOHN M. ALDRICH,	"
GEO. O. BRIGHAM,	Westboro'.
JONAS B. BRIGHAM,	"
THOMAS BROWN,	Worcester.
Miss SARAH D. BANCROFT,	"
JOHN S. BRIGHAM,	"
Miss SARAH M. BRIGHAM,	"
LEWIS F. BALL,	West Brookfield.
JOHN BARNARD,	Worcester.
Mrs. SARAH B. BARNARD,	"
WM. H. BROWN,	East Princeton.
ELLEN S. BROWN,	" "
WM. J. BAKER,	Worcester.
M. A. BARTLETT,	"
Miss P. A. BARNES,	"
Mrs. SARAH A. BUCKLEY,	Millbury.
WM. C. BARBOUR,	Worcester.
Mrs. M. A. BARBOUR,	"

Miss M. JENNIE BARBOUR,	Worcester.
CHAS. A. BARBOUR,	"
JAMES BROADBENT,	"
HENRY P. BARBOUR,	"
JOHN N. BANCROFT,	"
ELIAS T. BEMIS,	"
Mrs. E. T. BEMIS,	"
AZRO L. D. BUXTON,	"
MARY CONANT,	Barre.
Mrs. ELIZABETH S. CONNELL,	Troy, N. Y.
S. B. CORBIN,	Worcester.
JOSEPH CURTIS,	"
MARIA CURTIS,	"
E. W. CARTER,	"
Mrs. E. W. CARTER,	"
Miss ANNIE E. CHILDS,	"
LEMUEL COBURN.	"
Mrs. LEMUEL COBURN,	"
EDWARD I. COMINS,	"
HENRY CLAPP,	"
Rev. MR. COBB,	Northampton.
Mrs. MARTHA W. CHAMBERLAIN,	Worcester.
Miss CARRIE M. CHAMBERLAIN,	"
JOSIAH CHILDS,	Westboro'.
JAMES CLELAND,	Malden.
FRANK CORBIN,	Worcester.
THOS. W. DAVIS.	"
CHARLES DENNIS,	"
MARY DENNIS,	"
JOSEPH DAVIS,	"
Mrs. J. DAVIS,	"

J. T. EVERETT,	East Princeton.
Mrs. MARY A. EVERETT,	" "
Miss LIZZIE H. ELLIS,	Worcester.
G. W. ELKINS,	"
JAMES N. ENGLEY,	"
ARTHUR ESTABROOK,	Leicester.
Miss LIZZE A. FLAGG,	Worcester.
Miss REBECCA R. FAY,	"
E. EUGENE FORBES,	Westboro'.
GEO. A FORBES,	West Brookfield.
Mrs. M. ADELIA FORBES,	" "
ABRAHAM FAY,	Northboro'.
Mrs. ABIGAIL FAY,	"
WM. N. FIELD,	Worcester.
HIRAM FOBES,	"
THEO. N. GATES,	Westboro'.
Mrs. LIZZIE A. GATES,	"
Miss ABBIE A. GODDARD,	Worcester.
ORLANDO GODDARD,	"
Miss KATIE E. GATES,	"
BRAMAN GROUT,	Leicester.
FREDERICK GOULDING,	Worcester.
Mrs. A. W. GRANT,	Charlestown.
GEORGE GEER,	Worcester.
Mrs. HENRIETTA GEER,	"
WM. A. GREENE,	Shrewsbury.
SAMUEL GRIFFIN,	East Princeton.
MARY A. GRIFFIN,	" "
C. H. GOODWIN,	Worcester.
M. M. GARFIELD,	"
Mrs. LUCY M. GARFIELD,	"

Miss NELLIE H. GREENE,	Shrewsbury.
HENRY GLAZIER,	Worcester.
Mrs. MARIA H. GLAZIER,	"
JALAAM GATES,	"
WM. HUNT,	"
Mrs. WM. HUNT,	"
FREDERICK O. HARRINGTON,	"
JOHN HILLARD,	"
Mrs. ELIZA W. HILLARD,	"
FRANK E. HIGGINS,	"
ARTHUR H. HOWLAND.	"
S. A. HOWLAND,	"
JOHN HOMAN,	Westboro'.
C. S. HENRY,	"
CHENEY HATCH,	Leicester.
Mrs. CHENEY HATCH,	"
L. N. HOLTON,	Worcester.
Mrs. S. FRANCES HOLTON.	"
GIDEON HARRIS.	"
Mrs. SOPHIE R. HARRIS.	"
Miss RUTH A. HOWLAND,	"
N. C. HOWE,	"
Mrs. N. C. HOWE.	"
HENRY F. HARRIS.	Oakdale.
LINUS M. HARRIS.	"
Mrs. ARMILLA E. HARRIS,	"
WM. HARRINGTON,	Worcester.
F. G. HOOKER,	"
EZRA B. HOLMES,	"
SAMUEL D. HUBBARD,	Holden.
Mrs. E. C. HUBBARD,	"

ALBERT F. HATCH,	Worcester.
Mrs. SARAH R. HATCH,	"
FRANK A. HATCH,	"
HENRY H. HOLDEN,	"
Mrs. HENRY H. HOLDEN,	"
THEO. S. HOBBS,	"
Mrs. CLARA A. HOBBS,	"
Mrs. J. HUNT,	Vernon, Vt.
Miss MARY HALL,	Worcester.
WM. HENVILLE,	"
ISAAC JOHNSON,	Sturbridge.
Mrs. CHARLOTTE J. JOHNSON.	"
CHARLES H. JACKSON,	West Brookfield.
Mrs. CHARLES H. JACKSON,	" "
HENRY J. KENDALL,	Worcester.
Mrs. MARY J. KENDALL,	"
WM. KNOWLES,	"
Mrs. H. W. KNIGHTS,	Orange.
Mrs. E. M. KIMBALL,	Worcester.
ALBERT G. KENDALL,	"
Miss EMMA S. R. KENDRICK,	"
Mrs. LYDIA A. KINGMAN,	"
Miss ELDORA E. LORING,	Leicester.
Miss ABBIE L. LORING,	"
BETSEY MIDGLEY,	Lowell.
ALFRED C. MURRAY,	Worcester.
O. P. MAYNARD,	West Brookfield.
Mrs. M. L. MAYNARD,	" "
ALBERT H. MURDOCK,	West Boylston.
WM. MECORNEY,	Worcester.
Mrs. R. L. MECORNEY,	"

WM. MOORE,	Northboro.'
M. H. MIRICK,	East Princeton.
Mrs. L. M. MIRICK,	".. "
WALTER MOORE,	Worcester.
CHARLES MORSE,	"..
HENRY B. NOURSE,	Westboro'.
N. F. NEWELL,	Worcester.
Mrs. N. F. NEWELL,	"
CHARLES O. PARKER,	Westboro'.
Miss ELLA J. PRATT,	Worcester.
C. H. PIERCE,	Westboro'.
Mrs. E. E. PARKER,	Worcester.
ARTHUR D. PRATT,	"
Mrs. D. F. PARKER,	"
WM. D. PROUTY,	"
Mrs. WM. D. PROUTY,	"
Miss MARY E. PROUTY,	"
Miss ALICE M. PROUTY,	"
DEXTER H. PERRY,	"
DEXTER N. PRATT,	"
Miss SARAH F. PUTNAM,	"
Miss LOUISA M. RICE,	"
Miss HATTIE E. RICHARDS,	"
JOHN RICHARDS,	"
HENRY RICH,	"
HENRY F. ROSS,	"
Mrs. HATTIE E. RICH,	"
THOMAS STOTT,	"
Mrs. LEAH STOTT,	"
ALBERT J. STONE,	"
Mrs. BERT STONE,	West Brookfield.

GEORGE T. SCOTT,	Worcester.
Mrs. ELIZABETH S. SCOTT,	"
GEORGE SESSIONS,	"
Mrs. MARY J. SESSIONS,	"
Miss MARY S. SESSIONS,	"
DR. E. SCHOFIELD,	"
E. SMITH, Jr.,	"
Mrs. E. SMITH, Jr.,	"
Miss ESTELLA SMITH,	"
H. A. STREETER,	"
Mrs. H. A. STREETER,	"
Mrs. ALMOND STREETER,	"
Miss MARY SHAW,	Millbury.
P. H. SMITH,	Northampton.
T. H. STODDARD,	"
Miss HATTIE A. SMITH,	Worcester.
Miss S. ANNIE STEVENS,	"
Mrs. R. D. STEVENS,	Vernon, Vt.
Mrs. SWAIM,	Oxford,
S. D. TOURTELLOT,	Worcester.
Mrs. LUCY TOURTELLOT,	"
ELIAS TEMPLE,	"
Mrs. MARIA I. TAUNT,	"
Miss EMMA E. UPHAM,	"
C. N. WALKER,	"
Mrs. LIZZIE L. WALKER,	"
AMANDA L. WILCOX,	Uxbridge.
SAMUEL WARREN,	Holden.
MARION E. WARREN,	"
JAMES J. WARREN,	Brimfield.
Mrs. JAMES J. WARREN,	"

Miss FANNY E. WARREN,	Brimfield.
Miss ELLEN E. WARREN.	"
Miss MARY W. WARREN,	"
Master JOHN M. WARREN,	"
C. WARREN.	Leicester.
Mrs. SARAH A. WHITNEY,	Winchendon.
Miss KATE E. WHITE.	Leicester.
Miss MARIA J. WARREN,	"
Miss ADDIE J. WARREN,	"
SETH D. WILLIAMS.	Worcester.
DELUCAR S. WILLIAMS,	"
A. J. WARFIELD,	"
Mrs. A. J. WARFIELD,	"
Miss EMMA J. WOOD,	"
GEORGE W. WAKEFIELD,	"
A. G. WALKER,	"
A. L. WILLISTON.	Northampton.
HUGH A. WILLSON.	West Boylston.
CHAS. H. WOODWELL,	Worcester.
CLARENCE C. WHITE,	Leicester.
CORBIN O. WOOD.	Worcester.
Mrs. C. O. WOOD,	"
Miss H. WINSLOW.	Malden.
LEWIS F. WHITE,	Charlton Depot.
GEO. W. WHEELER,	Worcester.
Mrs. HARRIET S. WHEELER,	"
Miss MARY G. B. WHEELER,	"
Miss SARAH WILSON,	"

ORIGIN OF THE EXCURSION.

URING the summer of 1868, a party of worthy citizens from the "Heart of the Commonwealth," desiring to enjoy a season of recreation, organized themselves into an association by the choice of proper officers, and having chartered of Capt. W. W. Coit, of Norwich, Ct., the steamer bearing his name, they proceeded to said city August 3, and, taking possession of their "own hired boat," spent a few days in visiting Newport, Edgartown, New Bedford, etc. A further account of the trip may be found in a little volume of about the same size and style of this, entitled "By Sea and Land." Early this season, members of the same party, having pleasant recollections of the good time of last year, called a meeting of the "Coits," extending the invitation to others, the result of which was the organization of another party, retaining the old title "Coit Excursionists."

As there was a prospect of a much larger party, it became necessary to obtain a more capacious steamer than the one used last year, and after due consideration, the "*City of New London*" was chartered of Julius Webb, agent of the Boston, Norwich and New York Transportation Company, for an eight days' trip, an account of which will be found in the succeeding pages, made up of an extended article which appeared

2*

in the *Westboro' Chronotype*, whose editor, C. II. Pierce, Esq., was a member of the party, and a series of letters which appeared in the Worcester *Daily Spy* over the initials W. M.

Other matter was in the hands of your committee, but as it contains substantially the same facts, they did not think it would be advisable to publish it, neither did they feel at liberty to pass over the articles in the *Evening Gazette*, furnished that paper by the gentlemanly editor who was one of our party, without acknowledging their interest and worthiness of a place in this volume under other circumstances.

CRUISE OF THE COITS.

Originally published in the Westboro' Chronotype.

UGUST 11—18, 1869, are eight brilliant red-letter days in many a book of remembrance. They mark the grand carnival of pleasure prosecuted by two hundred and sixty ladies and gentlemen of Worcester and vicinity, over a water trip of seven hundred miles, and through eight cities. Much was anticipated from an excursion of such unusual proportions, but vastly more was realized. In fact, it proved the most successful affair of the kind which has yet been projected in New England.

The party was mainly made up of some of the best citizens of Worcester County; not people of wealth and social position merely, but those whose hearts are in the right place, and who never for a moment forget the amenities of life. Throughout the trip, starch was at a discount, and all stood upon a common level, mingling freely together as a "happy family;" and, what is a rather unusual circumstance, the Captain and one of the pilots joined unreservedly with the party wherever they landed, and at their evening entertainments. The Captain pronounced it the most agreeable and orderly party he ever took out; and one of the pilots emphatically assured me that he did not believe the affair could be beaten in any respect, and sincerely hoped to see us again next year.

The train which took us from Worcester gave up four cars, with a baggage car, to our exclusive use. These furnished rather limited quarters, and a few "set-a-standing," like the Dutchman's hen. We were not more than five minutes behind time in starting from Worcester, and reached Norwich at half past nine. The cars stopped within three or four rods of the pier; and before ten o'clock we were all on board the "*City of New London*," a fine steamer of 1203 tons.

The boat left the wharf at about ten o'clock, and the state-rooms were sold by auction immediately after. The sale was a lively competition throughout, prices being of little account to those with whom state-rooms were just then the things to be desired above all others. Forty-one rooms were sold at prices ranging from forty-two and a half down to eleven and a half dollars, aggregating eight hundred and ninety dollars. This made an average of $21.71,—nearly three times as much as the average prices obtained last year, and very materially reduced the general expenses of the trip. Geo. O. Brigham, of Westboro', bought a room for $25, and after the sale, was offered $40 for it. Another gentleman told me that he paid $12 for one, and had been offered $27 to give it up. Those who did not obtain state-rooms were afterwards provided with berths by lot. The party was then separated by lot into two divisions, each to alternate with the other in taking the first table at meals, as only one hundred and thirty could be seated at once. From each division a certain number volunteered or were detailed to wait upon the other table during each day.

The Commissary department was in excellent hands. Henry Glazier, of Worcester, was the steward, and soon got his feeding apparatus in good working order.

The inaugural day of the trip proved a magnificent one, although in the morning it looked a little unpromising. A thin haze obscured the sun, and a fresh, delightful breeze was stirring during most of the day. The boat moved as steadily through the waters of the Sound as a car upon the iron track, and not a soul on board had a thought of paying tribute to Old Neptune.

At four o'clock in the afternoon, we entered the harbor of New Haven, and in due time had reached the city of many elms and much learning. Our party was soon on shore, intent upon seeing as many of the sights as the limited time would permit. A few of us visited Yale College grounds, and rendered a verdict then and there, that during the vacation of the students, (as was then the case,) there is nothing specially attractive about the shades of academic groves and piles of brick a century old.

We delayed leaving New Haven till midnight. By this arrangement an excellent opportunity was afforded the party to view all the objects of interest along the approaches to New York city by daylight.

The trip up the East River and harbor was made in the early sunlight of a delightful day, which seemed to invest with a peculiar attraction the objects of note along the route. Breakfast was entirely forgotten in the absorbing business of gazing at and commenting upon the forts, the institutions on Blackwell's Island, the public buildings at other points, Hurl Gate and the operations in progress there for its removal, Jones' Wood, the Battery, and the water fronts of New York and Brooklyn. We reached Pier 40 at nine o'clock on Thursday morning.

The party now improved the few hours at command in such ways as seemed most desirable,—several of us visiting the far-famed Greenwood Cemetery, where over two hours were profitably spent in rambling through one of the most enchanting spots of consecrated ground in this country. It far surpasses Mount Auburn, beautiful as that cemetery is, although in the way of lot enclosures Greenwood is much behind the latter, which has discarded iron fences, and has substituted hammered granite borders.

The westerly entrance to the cemetery, which is approached by a very wide avenue, is a magnificent architectural structure in free-stone. The central portion, or carriage way, consists of two arches, over each of which, on each side, is a large and elaborately cut bas-relief, illustrating scriptural references to death and the resurrection. To the right and left are entrances for visitors on foot, and lobbies furnished with nicely upholstered double chairs.

In this cemetery is the famous monument to the memory of Charlotte Canda, who was killed on the seventeenth anniversary of her birth day. It was sculptured in Italy, in white marble. It is in the Gothic style, and in the

central arch is a statue of Charlotte Canda. It cost $70,-
000, (the bulk of the fortune Miss Canda would have
inherited,) and makes the smallest show for the money
expended that I have ever seen in a structure of this
character. The details are small and entirely fail to pro-
duce the effect of a bolder and less elaborate style. I was
informed that the remains of Miss Canda have been
removed from this costly resting place to another in the
city of Paris.

Another monumental structure worthy of note, is a life-
size statue of Captain Correga, in marble, standing upon
a granite pedestal. The Captain is represented as dressed
in citizen's garb, and wearing upon his head an old fashioned heavy topped fur cap. In his hands he holds a
sextant, with which he is taking an observation. This
statue was erected by the Captain himself, seventeen
years before his death. The instrument he holds is the
identical one used by him during his voyages, and was not
placed in position till after his death.

One of the chief objects of interest is the "Pilot's
Monument," situated on nearly the highest point of land in
the cemetery. and commanding a full and magnificent view
of the bay of New York. The monument was erected
by the New York City Government in perpetuation of

the memory of a pilot who lost his life several years ago while in the discharge of his hazardous duties.

Still another noticeable feature of this cemetery is the Firemen's Monument and surroundings, which are dedicated to the memory of the brave men who have sacrificed their lives in the discharge of their duty as firemen. The monument was erected by the Fire Department of the city of New York.

The style now somewhat in vogue here in the erection of family vaults, is to have them in two divisions,— a vestibule, and a series of sepulchral niches. The vestibule is reached through a door of open iron-work more or less ornamental. Opposite the door the wall of the vestibule is in panels of polished marble, nearly square, somewhat resembling a series of drawers, minus the handles. Each of these panels can be removed, and forms the head of a receptacle for a single coffin, which being deposited, the head or panel is sealed into its place, and the inscription placed upon it. Through the open-work of the door the passer-by can easily read all of these inscriptions. Sometimes vases of flowers are kept upon stands in the centre of the vestibule, and in one of them I saw a stand and two chairs, and on the former a work basket and contents.

Niblo, of theatrical fame, has recently erected a vault on

3

this plan, one of the most noticeable in the cemetery. The remains of his wife are there deposited, and on the panel which marks her resting place are the following pathetic lines:

> All that's beautiful in woman,
> All we in her nature love,
> All that's good in all that's human,
> Passed this gate to God above.

Several of the recently erected monuments are of granite with highly polished tablets, on which the inscriptions are cut. The polishing of the granite darkens the surface, and the contrast between this and the letters cut through it renders the inscriptions legible from any point of view. One very large monument has its entire surface polished, and is really one of the most impressive objects in the grounds.

It is altogether impossible to visit in two hours one half that is worth seeing in the four hundred and more acres of Greenwood Cemetery, or to give anything like an approach to a description of it in a newspaper article. A day might be spent in noting, and a book like this filled in describing, the many objects of interest within its limits.

In going to and returning from Greenwood Cemetery, our party visited that mammoth sink of filth and wretchedness, the Fulton Market. The stalls are unfit for Massachusetts hog pens, and the hucksters who occupy them are dirty and saucy. If, as the good Book intimates, there is any connection between cleanliness and godliness, one can not wonder at the depraved condition of the great city, after seeing this insufferable nuisance in its midst.

Of course no one goes to New York now without seeing Central Park; but most of our party postponed their visit to that place till their return to the city on Saturday.

At about four o'clock on the afternoon of Thursday we swung out from the pier, and commenced our royal trip up the Hudson River—the Rhine of America—whose legendary, historical and literary associations render doubly enchanting the grand and beautiful scenery along its banks. The great city stretches along the eastern shore for miles above our starting point; and on the opposite side lie Jersey City, Hoboken and Weehawken. Between the latter two places are the "Elysian Fields," a popular Sunday resort of the Germans, where music, dancing and lager beer prevail. Weehawken is noted as the scene of the fatal duel between Hamilton and Burr.

And now for miles and miles along the picturesque hights to the right appears an almost continuous succession

of stately mansions, with beautiful lawns, parks, gardens
and conservatories.   Here and there, too, are lovely sub
urban villages and thriving towns.   Among the points of
special interest in this section of the panorama, are the N.
Y. Lunatic Asylum; the house in which the Earl of
Devon lived; the house occupied by Joseph Bonaparte
while an exile in this country; that in which Audubon,
the celebrated Naturalist, lived and died; the N. Y. Deaf
and Dumb Institute; The site of Fort Washington; the
Roman Catholic Convent and Academy of Mount St.
Vincent; the castellated mansion built, but never occupied,
by Edwin Forrest; Yonkers, the home of Mary Phillips,
who might have wedded Washington had she been "will-
in';" the point from which Cornwallis crossed the river
in 1776 to capture Fort Lee; Dobb's Ferry, noted in
Revolutionary history as a place for the concentration and
encampment of troops—both British and American; and
where a British commission landed to intercede for the
life of Maj. Andre.

But while we have all this to charm and interest us
on the right, we have on the opposite shore that wonderful formation, the Palisades, whose precipitous fronts of
traprock rise like giant sentinels from three hundred to
five hundred feet in air, presenting one of the grandest

pictures of American scenery. They commence ten miles above our starting point, and continue more or less abruptly about fifteen miles.

We are now opposite Irvington, twenty-five miles from New York; and there, just north of the village, are the picturesque house and surroundings which constitute the world-renowned "Sunny Side," once the home of Washington Irving. Three miles farther on is Tarrytown, where stands in full view, overlooking the river, the "Paulding manor," built of white marble, and pronounced one of the finest specimens of Elizabethan architecture in this country. Just above us is the valley of "Sleepy Hollow," immortalized by Irving. Three miles above Tarrytown is the well known Sing Sing State Prison. The buildings are quite extensive and stand close to the water's edge. They are built of white marble, quarried in the vicinity—a material not commonly used in residences of this character. Opposite Sing Sing is Rockland Lake, from which 200,000 tons of ice are annually cut for the New York market.

The shades of evening have now settled down around us, and the balance of the trip to West Point is made by starlight. It is a warm, still, clear night; and the scenery through which we so quietly glide, instead of charming us

3*

as before with its details, now becomes impressive in its shadowy indistinctness.

Four miles above Sing Sing we pass Croton Point, off which the *Vulture* anchored when she brought Andre to meet Arnold, and where a gun was trained upon that vessel, and drove it down the river. Two miles more take us to Stony Point, a bold, rocky eminence, crowned by a light house, on the west side of the river. Here the stream is only half a mile wide, which fact, together with the commanding positions afforded by the neighboring hills, rendered this an important pass during the Revolution. Fortifications were erected here and at Verplanck Point opposite, and were the scenes of some hard fought battles. Very near Stony Point is "Treason Hill," and the house in which Andre and Arnold met and arranged the details for the surrender of West Point. Just above Stony Point, on the same side of the river, a lofty limestone cliff arises from near the water's edge; and at the foot of the cliff are the "Tomkins Lime Kilns," looking like a stone fortress.

We come now into the grandeur of a night scene upon the Hudson. After passing Stony Point, the river is narrow all the way to West Point, and soon the majestic Highlands begin. On either side are lofty peaks and rocky crags, which in the uncertain starlight seem to overhang the river within easy stone's throw of the spectator. Among these, on the left, is the long, ridge-like elevation, known as the "Donderberg," or Thunder Mountain, 1,000 feet high, and on the right is "Anthony's Nose," over 1,200 feet high. The former, according to a superstition recorded by Irving, was once peopled with a crowd of little imps in sugar loaf hats and short doublets, who "tumbled head over heels in the rack and mist," and brought down frightful squalls on such craft as failed to drop the peaks of their mainsails in salute to the Dutch goblin who kept the Donderberg. On the rocky hights opposite Anthony's Nose, stood forts Clinton and Montgomery, during the Revolution, and across the river was stretched a heavy boom,— a huge iron chain, on timber floats,— to prevent the upward passage of British vessels. In 1777 Sir Henry Clinton captured these forts and destroyed the boom.

On a commanding hight on the west side of the river is Cozzens' Hotel, brilliant with hundreds of lighted windows; and just above, and within a mile of West Point Landing, is the pier where, at nine o'clock, we made fast for the night.

At eight o'clock on Friday morning we cast off from

the pier, and moved up to West Point Landing. A
messenger had been sent forward with a request to permit our party to land and visit the grounds; but he at
first received a flat refusal, in conformity to a rule adopted
as a protection against the New York roughs and loose
women whose visits had become a nuisance. On being
informed, however, that we represented the eminent
gravity of Massachusetts, and had got West Point on
the brain, the commanding officer at once granted our
request.

The United States Military Academy buildings and
grounds occupy an area of about fifty acres, on a plateau
160 to 180 feet above the river. This plateau, or the
northeasterly corner of it, forms a projecting point, around
which the river makes a short turn to the left, and then
resumes its southerly course; and being on the west side of
the river its very appropriate name is West Point.

The grounds are reached from the landing by a steep
road cut in the rocky hillside. On the smooth, perpendic-
ular face of this cut, appears "Bunker Hill, 1775," in
deeply sunk letters nearly four feet high. It rather looked
to us like an attempt, on the part of New York, to steal
Massachusetts thunder.

To my mind, the most beautiful and interesting portion of the Hudson river is that which may be seen at one sweep of the eye about West Point, and for nine miles directly up the river. These views from the northerly extremity of the plateau contain as much of grandeur and historic interest as I expect ever to find in one landscape; and they well repaid me — and many others, I believe—for the entire expense of the trip. Before us is the river, with its smoothly gliding craft, its romantic islands and its winding shore beyond. To the north are the Highlands in all their glory, and between them stretches the river away to Newburgh, indistinctly seen at a distance of nine miles. At the northeast angle of the plateau, fully commanding this pass, is Fort Clinton, an earthwork thrown up in 1778, and on the extreme point is Roe's Hotel. Opposite the angle is Constitution Island, which was heavily fortified during the revolution; and remains of its old batteries may still be seen. A boom was also thrown across the river, between the island and the Point, consisting of an immense chain buoyed up on logs, each link of the chain weighing 120 lbs. A portion of the chain is still preserved here, and we afterwards saw three links of it at the Redwood Library in Newport.

To the west rises, as a back-ground, Mount Independence, far up whose rough precipitous side — nearly 600 feet above the river — stand the gray ruins of Fort Putnam; and at the base of the mountain, and looking out upon the Academy grounds through groves of shade trees, are the residences of the officers. At the southerly side of the plateau, and at right angles with the river, is the range of Academy buildings, attractive in their architecture and surroundings. The westerly half of the area thus enclosed is somewhat rolling, and is intersected with walks and dotted with fine shade trees. The easterly portion is the parade ground, and is about as level as a floor.

Among the objects of interest are the monument and garden of Kosciusko; and the monumental statue of Major General Sedgwick, who fell at Spottsylvania, and for whom the Grand Army post in Westboro' is named. The statue is in bronze, standing on a granite pedestal, and represents the General in full military dress and attitude. In a grove of elms are several trophy guns, which were captured during the revolution, the war of 1812–15, the Mexican war, and the late rebellion.

The whole neighborhood abounds with interesting military associations. Here it was that in 1780, Benedict Arnold, of hated memory, assumed command, and soon after sought to betray his trust. On the opposite shore is the house he occupied as headquarters, and where he received the news of Andre's capture. Near it, in the bank of the river, is a little cove, whence Arnold started in his hasty flight to the *Vulture*, which lay below, leaving his wife to entertain the unsuspecting Washington. Here were educated many traitors of our own time—among them Robert E. Lee, Beauregard, the two Johnsons and others; but here, too, were trained up for the future salvation of the Republic, brave and faithful officers like Grant, Sherman, Sheridan and many others.

There are about 250 cadets here now, and their education costs the government five thousand dollars each. They were in camp when we were there, as they always are during the months of July and August.

Shortly after our arrival there was an artillery drill and practice-firing by the famous Reno Battery. Firing during the evolutions had been omitted for about a fortnight, but was practised to-day for our special entertainment. The precision with which the various movements of this battery are performed by both men and horses, is something remarkable, the latter seeming to understand the bugle calls by which the orders are given, fully as well as the men.

There was also some target firing from the water battery north of the Point. The target was stationed across the bend in the river, and the balls could be distinctly seen to strike in the bank behind it. Each discharge of the gun was followed by one of the most singular echoes mortal man ever heard. It is caused by the hights and valleys which skirt the river above, and sounds very much like *rip-rip-rip-rip*, a dozen times sharply and quickly repeated.

At ten o'clock we returned to the boat, and proceeded on our upward trip. After passing the double bend in the river, forming the Point, we came into the heart of the Highlands, which rise abruptly on either side, from twelve hundred to fifteen hundred feet in hight. Among the tallest of these peaks are Cro'-Nest, the Storm King, Mount Taurus, Butter Hill and Break-Neck Hill. On the northerly slope of the Storm King is "Idlewild," the home of the late N. P. Willis.

We made no stops after leaving West Point, till we reached the city of Hudson, the farthest point of our trip, at half-past four o'clock P. M.

The arrival at Hudson of such an expedition as ours, came very near astonishing the natives. In an extended notice of the event the Hudson *Star* of the next morning spoke of "the large and beautiful Sound steamer, *City of New London*, which made its unexpected appearance in the channel opposite the city yesterday afternoon, creating quite an excitement; for never before in our remembrance has a vessel of this class landed at our docks or passed up the river."

We had between three and four hours to spend in Hudson, and nearly all of our party improved the time in looking about the place. Most of us walked, but Capt. G. H. Power, a prominent citizen, hastily mustered two or three carriages and placed them at the disposal of as many of our party as they would accommodate. The officers of our expedition were assured by the Mayor of the city, that had he known of our coming we should have had a reception worthy of the occasion.

Hudson is a quaint old Dutch town, (or "city,") 115 miles from New York. It was named after Hendrick Hudson, who discovered the noble river on which it stands, and who supposed, till after he passed this point, that he had found the long-sought "Northwest Passage" to India. It was incorporated as a city eighty-four years ago, and there are but four charters in the State which ante-date it. The population stands at about 8,000, and there it has probably stood for the last fifty years. It is

4

only a few miles from the traditional scene of Rip Van
Winkle's long nap; and it seems as though the same
sleepy spell had brooded over the city ever since.

Of the churches here, two are very fine and nearly new,
one being of freestone, and one of pressed brick; but
most of the buildings have an ancient, dull look; on the
principal business street, as elsewhere, they are mainly
two-story wooden structures. The only hotel I saw looked
very like an unpretentious country tavern; and one bar-
ber's shop and one three-cent news stand, were the
reward of my long search for those land-marks of civili-
zation.

Just north of the landing is a bluff nearly 100 feet above
the river; and on its summit is a public square and promenade, handsomely laid out and ornamented with trees and
shrubbery. From this look-out we had a charming view
of the river below, and of the country along the opposite
shore, with the picturesque Catskill Mountains as a back-
ground. A portion of the city rises to a still greater
hight than this plateau.

At about sunset the steamer swung off into the channel
and our homeward trip commenced. As we moved away
we made the hills echo with cheers for the city, and for
Capt. Power and others, which were responded to by the

crowds on the wharves and Promenade Hill, with steam whistle accompaniments from the workshops and locomotives near the river. A party of boys who were preparing to bathe in one of the docks, hastily completed the disrobing process, and joined in the general commotion by swinging their shirts aloft and dancing and yelling with desperate energy.

The *Star* says, in concluding the article before referred to: "The whole affair was of so pleasant a character that it will be long remembered by those who had the pleasure of being spectators."

After a delightful moonlight ride of four hours, we reached the wharf at Poughkeepsie and made fast for the night. During this passage, many of the party passed the time on the decks in singing snatches of songs, and in conversation and games, while others made themselves comfortable in the cabin below, with cards, stories and the piano.

Soon after daylight Saturday morning, we took a stroll about town.

Unlike Hudson, Poughkeepsie is a wide-awake, thriving place. It has been incorporated as a city but fifteen years; yet the population is more than twice that of Hudson. The bulk of the city is built on a table land 150 to 200 feet above the river, with a slope more or less steep to the river bank. Next the river the streets are dirty and unattractive, but as they go back to higher ground they rapidly improve. Many of them are ornamented with fine shade trees. I passed through two or three streets, the carriage-ways of which were completely over-arched by double rows of tulip poplars.

Here are some of the finest mansions in the State, and the extensive grounds surrounding them are thrown open to the public.

Several important manufacturing establishments are located here — one of them the famous Vassar Brewery. Vassar is dead, but his name will be perpetuated by the extensive female college, standing in the easterly part of the city, and which was founded and endowed by his munificent liberality.

There are other noted educational institutions here, among them Eastman's Commercial College, one department of which a few of us visited, and saw some of the largest pen drawings ever executed.

South of the city is the residence of S. F. B. Morse, the inventor of the telegraph.

At eight o'clock, having taken in a fresh supply of milk and green corn, in exchange for three or four delinquent members of our company, we left Poughkeepsie, and in two hours reached the charming little city of Newburgh, on the west side of the river.

The great centre of attraction at Newburgh is an old stone house which Washington occupied as his head-quarters during the latter part of the revolution; and we visited it in full force. The property is owned and kept in order by the State of New York. The house stands on a lofty terrace, facing the river, of which there is an un-obstructed view. Cannon are planted on the lawn in front, and near by is a flag-staff, and a brownstone monument in memory of Uzall Knapp, the last of Washington's Life Guards.

One of the rooms of this venerable building was used by Washington for the transaction of business; here he issued his proclamation for the cessation of hostilities, March 19th, 1783; and here, on the third of November following, he disbanded the American army. In the cen-tre of a room is a stick of timber pointed with iron, which was part of a *cheveaux de frise* sunk in the river in 1780, to prevent the passage of British war sloops; here, too, are antique guns of monstrous length, swords, knap-sacks, saddles, wooden canteens, an old battle flag, conti-

4*

nental dresses; and a cocked hat worn by Robert Waugh from 1760 to 1816.

In another room is a case containing a collection of old books, continental money, powder horns, part of a musket used and broken at Bunker Hill, and many other articles. Hanging against the wall is a Hessian officer's boot of curious proportions — the length of leg being 14 inches, its circumference, both at top and ankle, $21\frac{1}{4}$ inches, and bottom of heel $4\frac{3}{4}$ inches across. Near it hangs a captured scarf of Santa Anna. Here, too, under the old fashioned, enormous stone chimney, hangs an ancient tea kettle, which once did duty for the Father of his Country. In the third room is a lock of Washington's hair and a piece of his coffin, his military orders, proclamations, rolls, and other documents; also, an ancient sofa, and the piano of Gen. Clinton, the first ever brought into Orange County.

Those of our party who were left behind at Poughkeepsie here rejoined us, and we proceeded on our way to New York, arriving there at five o'clock P. M.

No Puritanical scruples concerning Saturday night amusements hamper the New York conscience, and the theatres are in full blast on that evening. Being among the

Romans, nearly 150 of us ventured to do as the Romans do, and "went in." We visited Booth's new theatre, whose imposing exterior of hammered New England granite is eclipsed by its gorgeous interior finish, decorations and upholstery. It is a Dramatic Palace, and probably has no superior in this country.

The play was "Rip Van Winkle,"—an appropriate finale to our Hudson River trip. It was having a great "run" at the time we were there, with Joseph Jefferson as the principal character. It was specially written for him by Bourcicault; and his consummate impersonation of the easy, good-natured, good-for-nothing Dutchman, must fully realize the author's conception of the character. Says a critic: "From first to last he portrays, with exquisite touches of humor and pathos, a character which is unfortunately too familiar to us in the common walks of life ; and succeeds in showing the truly human elements of a tender, loving nature under all the squalor, debasement and wretchedness of a dissipated career." No other actor attempts this version of the legend, as indeed no other can, the play being controlled by copy-right.

Sunday in New York! Its sights and sounds are enough to set a straight-laced Massachusetts man's teeth on edge. Before our somewhat late breakfast was over, well filled excursion steamers were sailing gaily past us, bound for Hoboken, the Elysian Fields, Coney Island and other Sunday resorts. Their passengers, I should judge, were not particularly eminent for piety. Bands of music were on board, and on the upper deck of one of the boats were several cotillon sets in full swing, under the inspiration of some excellent but rather profane music.

Religious services were held on our steamer day and evening, which were well attended; but many of our party thought their opportunity for seeing Sodom in its Sunday clothes, ought to be improved, and governed themselves accordingly.

Here and there, in convenient places, a game of base ball or some other equally devotional exercise was in progress; drinking saloons and Jew clothing shops were driving a thrifty business; and in some sections of the city fruit stands were almost as frequent as the street corners.

During the afternoon and evening a large majority of our party visited Central Park, the great popular Sunday resort of both citizens and strangers; and no better investment of time or money can be made by sight-seers than in riding over its broad, smooth, winding avenues, strolling through its cozy, retired walks, or inspecting its costly and elaborate works of art, principal among which are the Bridges and Terrace.

The park is two and a half miles long and half a mile wide, and contains 862 acres, nearly one fourth of which is water. The two reservoirs contain 142 acres, and the Lake, one of the most attractive features of the landscape, contains twenty acres. There are nine and a half miles of carriage roads, five and a half miles of bridle roads and twenty-seven miles of walks.

Here at least the banditti horde, known as hackmen, who prey upon the public with their swindling charges, are kept at bay. Carriages owned and run by the city, and capable of seating twelve persons, make regular trips around the Park. It requires about an hour and a half to complete the circuit, and the very reasonable fare is twenty-five cents. If the driver is loquacious, as ours was, he will call attention to points of special interest. At the upper end of the Park we had a view of the celebrated High Bridge at Harlem.

The City also provides boats at the Lake, which will take you the circuit of its romantic, winding shore for ten cents. On our trip we passed several bridges, under one of which the oarsman gave the gunwale of the boat a smart rap with his oar, and the echo sounded like the report of a pistol.

Opposite the Park, at the corner of Seventh Avenue and Fifty-ninth street, is the "Central Park Garden," consisting of a large concert hall, from which a drinking saloon opens on one side, a smoking room on the other, and a "Garden" in the rear. The garden is of somewhat limited area, and contains a fountain, a little shrubbery, two tiers of stalls, and some tables and chairs. Concerts of instrumental music are given here every evening of the week, and on Sunday afternoon, by Theodore Thomas's unrivalled band; and the delightful strains can be listened to in the hall, or from the garden. The hall is also provided with tables; and the bibulously inclined can have their brandy and a straw, or a whisky straight, brought to them either in the hall or the garden, by one of the waiters in attendance. This way of spending Sunday would not be warmly encouraged in Westboro', but in New York they think differently.

We left New York at midnight, bound for Newport. Our route lay outside of Block Island, and early in the forenoon the long roll of the sea, "right from Europe," was reached. Trouble now commenced; and for awhile the rebellious stomachs of about one half the party had it all their own way. Some of the victims spitefully pitched their recent breakfasts overboard, while others only laid back and looked unutterable things. After two or three hours of this "sport,"—(it *was* sport to some of us,)—we came to smoother water, and all on board enjoyed a lovely sail up Newport harbor. As we passed Lime Rock, the home of the heroine, Ida Lewis, that famous lady made her appearance, and waved a welcome with her handkerchief. Of course we replied as gallantly as we knew how. At half past two in the afternoon we reached the wharf.

A large number of our party immediately chartered some sail boats, (which generally lay at the wharf, waiting for such jobs,) and hastened off to Lime Rock to pay their respects to Ida Lewis.

The "Rock," which rises out of the water in the southerly part of the harbor, is a very small affair. The only dwelling upon it,—and in fact the only one for which there is any room,—is that which Ida's father occupies; and this constitutes a portion of the "light-house," of which he is the keeper.

It was from this rock that the heroine put off in her boat to the rescue of drowning men—eleven in all, on five different occasions: the first being about ten years ago, when she was eighteen years old, and the last in March of this year.

Near the landing is a boat-house, overhanging the water, in which is kept the boat built for and presented to Miss Ida as a testimonial to her heroism. The boat is an elegant affair, and "they say" its owner can handle the oars with grace and vim.

Ida has an eye to business, by keeping on hand a supply of photographs, of which we each bought a copy; and some who received a piece of scrip from Ida's hand, in change, tucked it carefully away, as a more valuable keepsake than the picture. Many also picked up and brought away fragments of stone with which the rock is strewn.

Before returning to the steamer, we were taken over to Fort Adams. This is one of largest fortifications in Uncle Samuel's dominions, and mounts some very heavy guns. It is connected by a subterranean passage with a redoubt in the rear, so that in case of necessity the garrison can make a safe retreat and blow up the fort. Some of our party traversed this passage, which has to be done in a stooping posture. On coming out of the fort we passed the guard house, where a victim of military despotism was pining behind a grated door. How we pitied that poor fellow! but we were powerless to help him, and could only shake our fists in indignation at the U. S. Government for this undeserved treatment of one of its faithful defenders. I say "undeserved," because we had it from the victim's own lips that he "hadn't done nothing."

Newport is noted chiefly as a resort of fashion during the "heated term." There are some fine hotels here, besides private cottages, at which this class of patrons is supplied with all the luxuries of refinement and wealth. The principal hotels are the Ocean and Atlantic Houses, on Bellevue Avenue. The former is of magnificent proportions, with a broad and lofty portico, in which the "*ton*" delight to lounge. Directly in front of this portico is a showy band stand, which is occupied every pleasant afternoon, during the season, by first-class musicians. We had the good luck to hear Gilmore's band, led by Arbuckle.

The great attraction at Newport is Bellevue Avenue, which is lined with elegant residences, and in the latter part of the afternoon swarms with "tourn-outs" of every description, from the majestic family carriage drawn by "four-in-hand," bedizened with trimmings, and attended by liveried lackeys, down to the smallest basket phæton, more or less nobby in style. The coachmen and footmen of

all these tourn-outs sit bolt upright; the latter with folded
arms, as dignified as Julius Cæsar, especially if they
happen to belong to the African persuasion. A new
road has been built along*by the beach, in continuation
of the Avenue, which makes a very excellent and attractive drive. Six dollars gave five of us a ride over this
Avenue and back, and we saw that worth of the elephant.

Among the other features of interest in this city, are
the Beach, almost as hard and smooth as a floor; the old
Stone Mill, so called, an odd-looking structure in Touro
Park, whose origin and use are a mystery; the statue of
Commodore Perry; the Jewish Cemetery, with its massive
stone gateway; the Redwood Library, and the State House.

On Tuesday afternoon we steamed down to Rocky Point
for a clam-bake; but as no provision had been made for
such a crowd, some of us do not know to this day what
a baked clam tastes like. We had a fine trip, though,
and enjoyed the romantic surroundings of the Point much.

Our last evening on the boat, as we laid at the wharf,
was spent in a most social and agreeable manner. One
of the features was the introduction of a new variety of
pears — a pair of black babies, — in a nicely covered
basket. During the evening, several complimentary resolutions were passed, and an original hymn was read and

sung, all which are published in another part of this book.

At midnight we sailed for New London; and after looking that place over an hour or two, proceeded to Norwich, reaching the wharf in one hour short of seven days from the time we left it outward bound. As we passed up the river an old lady stood at her door, and swung her liege lord's nether garment as a "welcome home."

Before landing we gave a series of blow-out cheers for the Grand Carnival of Pleasure and everybody and everything connected with it.

C. H. PIERCE.

LETTERS

Originally published in the Worcester Daily Spy.

STEAMER "CITY OF NEW LONDON,"

New Haven, August 11, 1869.

WE promised the friends we left behind that they should hear from us through the medium of the *Spy*. We took an early start this morning from your, our, dear old city, and made the trip by rail to Norwich, on time. Our friend Turner, the agent, had made ample accommodations for the party, and was attentive to our wants until we had passed into the hands of the faithful conductor of the train. We reached our steamer about nine A. M., and found all things in readiness for us, with the officers on board ready to receive us, and make our trip pleasant.

We found the steamer in excellent condition; we could ask for nothing more satisfactory. We have plenty of room, although our company is what would be called large for an eight-day excursion trip. We number over two hundred and sixty; and have come to the conclusion that we have a first-rate company. We have over sixty persons outside of the city of Worcester, representing the towns of Northampton, Northboro', Holden, Charlton, Uxbridge, West Boylston, Leicester, Whitinsville, Millbury, West Brookfield, etc. The oldest man among the company is Cheney Hatch, of Leicester, the quarter-of-a-century cashier of Leicester Bank. The youngest man, I should think from appearance, is G. W. Wheeler, our city treasurer. At any rate I should judge that most of the company were living over their young days. If one day's trip on the salt water has such a renovating effect, I know not what may be expected when the eight days are up. We certainly have a good natured company. The trip on the steamer to this place was truly delightful. We all enjoyed it very much, and not a "sea-sick" soul could be found among the company. We reached the delightful "City of Elms" about five this afternoon. Of course we all must take a look at the place, to admire its beauty.

There is no particular event worth recording, except the immense excitement caused by the sale at auction of our state-rooms. The crowd around our auctioneer, Glazier, was immense. We could not realize that money

5*

was so plenty and business so brisk, after leaving Worcester so lately. The "bridal chamber" was first offered. It brought the small sum of $40. Although there were several lately married couples present, the room was taken by one of our Worcester friends who had the matrimonial knot tied years ago. The last room sold brought $42.50. The lucky buyer was from Northampton. We realized about $1,000 from state-rooms. We defy the great Erie railroad Fisk to beat this. He has found a rival this time.

Now, dear friends at home, we will close by saying to you that we are all right, and hope to go ahead as well as we have begun. We stay here over night, and to-morrow morning we expect to wake up in New York city, to have a look at the Park and other wonderful sights of that heated city.

You shall hear from us daily, if the *Spy* is willing.

W. M.

West Point, N. Y., August 13.

THE steamer *City of New London* has reached this place with the "Coit Excursionists" all right. We prolonged our stay at New Haven somewhat, and concluded to give Bridgeport the go-by in order to reach New York city early Thursday morning. It was the first trip of many of our party to this noted city, strange as it may seem to hundreds of your readers who make frequent visits to Gotham during the year.

We arrived in New York at nine A. M. on the 12th inst., and, notwithstanding the scorching atmosphere, landed and proceeded in force to Central Park. We "did" the park thoroughly, and, as far as members are concerned, the heart of your old Commonwealth was never better represented there before. We returned to the steamer at four P. M., laden with peaches and ready for our trip up the Hudson. New York is flooded with peaches, — larger, finer, superior everyway to the things that are sold for peaches in Worcester, and they are very much cheaper, too. *Genuine* peaches, luscious and beautiful, were selling at 75 cents and $1.00 per bushel.

Our sail up the Hudson river was delightful. I will

not attempt a description of the magnificent scenery. Hundreds have attempted to do so, but all have failed to do the subject justice. Those of our party who have made this trip before, found the Hudson river scenery more beautiful than ever before. Those who are here for the first time wonder why all Worcester does not hasten to New York to make this charming voyage. We had intended to tarry one night at West Point, but the authorities here who have been much annoyed by excursion parties, in the past, have put a stop to such visitations, and now refuse to allow any excursion boats or parties to land at their wharf. The commander, however, consented to let us take a view of the premises. I need not attempt to give a description of the place, or what "Uncle Sam" is doing here to train the young "how to shoot." Every one understands the matter better than I do. Suffice it to say, that a more delightful or appropriate place for the military academy could not have been found. Our whole party came to the conclusion, after a visit to this place, that it was worth the whole trip to have seen West Point and view the scenery, and witness the dress parade of the cadets. We think they excel even our State Guard in military evolutions. We stopped but a few hours, having previously landed for the night about two miles below here.

We found Hudson a very pretty place. It contains about 8,000 inhabitants, who appeared to regret very much that they had not been informed that we were to pay them a visit; they desired to give us a public reception. One generous and public spirited man, named George H. Power, came aboard as soon as we touched the landing place, and, though a stranger to all of us, furnished us which two carriages in which to ride about the place. We spent the next night at Poughkeepsie, before leaving which place we bought some cans of milk and a cart load of green corn. As we have two doctors on board, our friends at home deed not be alarmed.

Our rations, under the direction of friend Glazier, our steward, are ample in quality and quantity. We are living high, and sleeping all around. Our evenings are among the happiest of our hours. We are rich in musical talent, and, have also a great variety of speaking talent. Then of course we have some harmless amusements for the young. On the whole, we think we have made a decided improvement on last year's trip. In fact, we are already contemplating an excursion, next year, to *Europe!* Our experience will give us advantage over "green hands!"

I have no cases of "sea sickness" to report as yet; but next Monday night, look out for this part of the programme. At that time we shall probably have passed Point Judith, on our way to Newport.

By the way, in the list of towns represented in the "Coit Excursion," Westboro' should not have been left out.. There are eleven from that place, who have be‑ haved, so far, exceedingly well, and could not be spared from the party.   W. M.

On board "City of New London,"
New York, August 14, 1869.

WE left Poughkeepsie this forenoon about eight o'clock; we found the place quite a thriving city; there are many places of note, all of which your readers are familiar with; therefore I make no attempt at description of what we saw there. Perhaps I ought to mention Vassar college; many of our party paid a visit to this celebrated place; they describe it as very beautiful and extensive. I only saw the lager beer brewery where the money was made that built the college. The brewery is certainly very extensive, and I should judge that about as much misery might come from this brewery as good would come from the college. Perhaps the man's conscience is very much eased by the fact that although he may get his money in a mean way, he is giving it for good purposes; in other words, attempting to serve God and the devil at one and the same time.

Perhaps I may be wandering from my subject, which is an attempt to give a description of our journey from place to place, as well as incidents of travel. We stopped for about two hours this forenoon at Newburgh, a very interesting place about sixty miles from New York city. Our party visited what was once the headquarters of General Washington. The building is situated on a high point of land, commanding a beautiful view of the Hudson and the scenery surrounding it. Here in this venerable building is found much that would interest the historian as well as the lover of the "father of his country," the beloved Washington. It was here that Washington proclaimed the cessation of hostilities, March 19th, 1783, and disbanded the American army November 3d, 1783. Here are found

Washington's chair, written orders to his army, a lock of his hair, a piece of his coffin, his looking-glass,—in fact, a great variety of articles which doubtless once belonged to him.. We came back to our steamboat, feeling that we had added another link to the chain of memory that makes this trip one of the most pleasant occasions of our history.

We made no other landing on the Hudson. We are all delighted with the trip on the river. All agree that we could not have selected any other route that would have pleased us all so well as this. It is a fortunate affair that the committee of arrangements have been so fortunate as to please a company of two hundred and sixty or more people.

We arrived at pier No. 40, New York city, at five o'clock this afternoon; here we expect to have our steamer "made fast" until Monday morning, at which time we start for Newport. Our company scattered themselves pretty generally through the city, about as soon as we were fairly landed, some to see dear friends, others to see the sights, others, we should judge by the way they came back loaded, to get peaches, melons, pears, and other good things to eat. For the credit of the whole company, let me now say, that I have not seen or smelt a drop of intoxicating liquor since we started from home, among our company. I take great pride in publishing this fact to the world, and especially to that part of it who think it necessary to use it as a medicine, or in order to enjoy a social excursion. We know, or think, that a pleasanter or happier party cannot be found.

W. M.

Steamer "City of New London,"
New York, August 15, 1869.

NEW YORK cannot be looked upon as a desirable place in which to spend a hot, uncomfortable Sunday. With its dust and turmoil, its endless excitement, and constant flow of brain-crazing experience and incident, the vast metropolis cannot be viewed, even on week days, as an inviting point for pleasure seekers, such as form our goodly company. Had our committee of arrangements been able to foresee the height to which the mercury would attain, this portion of our time would, doubtless, have been spent in some cooler port. However, the cruise, thus far, has been fraught with so much of real pleasure for all our company, that we willingly overlook the discomforts of our experience here.

This morning, religious services, of a most interesting nature, were held on board our steamer, conducted by our chaplain, Rev. G. J. Sanger, assisted by Rev. Mr. Cobb, of Northampton; the presence of both of which gentlemen in our midst has added much to the charm of our voyage. Chaplain Sanger, basing his discourse on the most poetical text: "O, that I had the wings of a dove; I would fly away and be at rest."—Ps. lxv.: 6,—preached a most excellent and appropriate sermon. Remembering that his hearers had sought, in thus leaving their homes and business in the old Commonwealth, a few days of enjoyment in rest from their accustomed labors, the speaker grasped the idea, and made the central thought of his address the true rest for which the soul of man craves, and how that rest may be found. A report of the sermon would hardly be in place here, but it was a most pleasing discourse for the listeners.

The musical portions of the exercises were conducted by Mr. G. W. Elkins, of Worcester, while Miss Emma

Upham presided at the piano. This, as may well be judged, formed a most pleasing feature of the services. At the close of these Sabbath exercises, nearly all of our party went on shore, ostensibly to attend the city churches. The "smartest" and most popular clergymen, and the most magnificent church edifices were sought by many; but, in many cases, the houses of worship were found closed, and the would-be attendants found their way to Central Park and other points of interest about the city. In these warm days the morals of the metropolis, never too good, are left to run themselves, while the spiritual advisers, following in the footsteps of Rev. Mr. Murray and other pleasure seekers, with valise, gun and fishing rod, travel off to the Adirondacks, or, more soberly inclined, quietly rusticate by the seaside.

As we walked over the city, we found quite a number of stores open, while the grogshops seemed driving an excellent business. This will, doubtless, sound strange to Massachusetts ears, as it looked strange to our Massachusetts eyes. It might reasonably be judged that the class of people in New York who usually attend church on the Sabbath, have, either followed the footsteps of their pastors and "taken a vacation," or, in the absence of their preachers, degenerated into Sabbath breakers.

Lager beer saloons were crowded with thirsty customers; steamers, laden with pleasure-seekers, sailed up and down the river, bound to shore resorts or to the banks of the Hudson; bands of music could be heard, and dancing parties seen on the decks of these steamers, as they bore their thoughtless burdens of New York's men and women out over the waters; ball clubs were found playing "the national game," even in some of the public streets; while ferry boats, steam cars, horse cars, and omnibuses, all loaded to their fullest extent, presented scenes which might well appear strange to our party, reared as they had been with such different views of life's duties, and of the Sabbath and its observance.

We do not claim perfection for the old Bay State, but we certainly believe that her customs and her record of daily life do not savor so strongly of the "pit" as do those of Gotham. In spite of the corruption manifest on every hand, we have endeavored to sustain the name and credit of our honored city and State.

Gathering on our steamer at night, we again joined in religious services. Rev. Mr. Cobb preached a practical sermon, which was listened to with deep interest by his hearers, from the text: "Be careful for nothing,"—Phil. vi.: 4;—and he presented many truths with force and distinctness, which, if applied to our daily manner of living, might work much good. The evening services were a fit and pleasing close for the events of the day.

Taking all things together, in spite of the oppressive heat and the discomforts of the day, we shall assuredly mark this as one of the most interesting and profitable thus far spent. It is our intention now to cast off from New York at midnight to-night, and, if wind and weather prove fair, you will soon hear from us, with our steamer anchored in Newport harbor.

W. M.

STEAMER "CITY OF NEW LONDON."

Newport, August 16, 1869.

RIGHT glad were our party to leave the city of New York. We certainly shall not wish to stop again over Sunday in hot weather at a New York dock. We left there soon after midnight, this morning; the weather, we found, had suddenly changed, or we had been near that hot place we read of. The sailing was fine and delightful; all were as gay as larks and as hungry as

6*

sharks, waiting as patiently as possible for breakfast. We all had eaten a very hearty meal, and we could see the squint in the steward's eye, as much as to say, you won't keep that breakfast long. The party crowded to the front part of the deck to view the ocean scenery, and also to keep an eye on those that might first give in to the rising of the waves and the rocking and rolling of the boat. Soon it was observed that now and then one of the party would begin to grow pale about the mouth; then, soon, a zig-zag movement towards the railing of the boat to *look* over; then some friend would step up to hold the head gently over the railing, then ———; it was then time for the well ones to shout, sing, and laugh; this was kept up for about an hour and a half, the squad at the side of the boat increasing in numbers, till nearly all the party had successfully gone through the usual exercises on such interesting occasions. So few were unaffected that for a while it was difficult to find persons enough to hold the heads over the side. This state of things lasted for two long hours; soon after the steward brought up a few bushels of crackers, with plenty of tea and coffee, and the trouble was over; we resumed our several places, and "Richard was himself again." Well, it might have been interesting to the lookers-on to witness the scene, but it was anything but fine to the participants. It is no easy matter to describe "sea sickness;" it can be better *felt* than described.

We arrived in this place about half-past two o'clock this P. M. Newport is full; the hotels are full; the usual amount of flirting and snobbing are seen; the splendid turn-outs and drives may be seen on the avenue in the early evening. Many of our party hired carriages and took a drive "around the new road," which is about nine miles. It is a very pleasant ride of about two hours as the hacks drive here, and it is very fine; most of the magnificent residences of the place are found on this road. People who come here have not gone through the programme till they have been over this road.

We leave to-morrow for Rocky Point for a clam bake, and return here in the afternoon to stop over night. Wednesday morning we leave for "sweet home." We have a party with us from Princeton who should not be omitted from the record. As we become more acquainted with each other the attachments are stronger; and we have none in our party we would like to part with till our excursion is over, and the time comes for us to return to our usual avocations.   W. M.

HOME AGAIN!

WORCESTER, August 18.

T home again! We are gratified at the great success of the excursion. We took our departure
from Newport at an early hour this morning, and arrived
at the picturesque city of Norwich at about 9 A. M.
Here we made a stop for two hours or more before
proceeding further on our homeward journey, and finally
reached Worcester at half-past two in the afternoon.

Of course we could not break up this large and interesting party without expressing our gratitude to some of those
who had contributed to the success of our excursion.
Last night we had our farewell meeting in the cabin, which
was crowded to its utmost capacity. For three hours we
made speeches, told stories and sang. The literary and
musical talent of our party was fairly developed, and in the
evening manifestations ranged from grave to gay. The
merriment was increased when one gentleman produced
the basket of pears that had been demanded of him. The
largest "pair" consisted of a couple of little colored chil-

dren who had been snugly hid away in the bottom of the basket. The committee on resolutions reported the following:

Whereas, We, members of the Coit Excursion party— not unmindful of Him who constantly watches over us, and to whom we are indebted for life and all its pleasures— having had a glorious time during our present excursion, feel that the promoters of our enjoyment deserve some expression of our appreciation of their efforts in our behalf, therefore

Resolved, That our unfeigned thanks and heart-felt gratitude are due to Mr. George R. Peckham, our worthy president, through whom we have been furnished with our intellectual entertainments; Mr. William Mecorney, our faithful clerk and reporter; Mr. Geo. W. Wheeler, our treasurer, who accepts the responsible position of receiving and paying out our money, besides otherwise contributing largely to the pleasure of our party; Mr. Henry Glazier, our faithful steward, who has *successfully* and *satisfactorily* provided for our tables, and exercised a constant watchfulness that all should be cared for; and all other officers of our party for their efforts in our behalf.

Resolved, That the Rev. Mr. Sanger, for his faithful services as chaplain and excellent discourse on Sabbath morning, and the Rev. Mr. Cobb, for his interesting and practical address on Sabbath evening, have endeared themselves to us, and will long be remembered.

Resolved, That our thanks are due to Dr. Edwin Schofield, for his faithful attention to those who have needed his professional services during the excursion.

Resolved, That we duly appreciate the efforts of Mr. Elkins, Mr. and Mrs. Maynard, Miss Winslow, Miss Warren, and others of our party who have contributed to our enjoyment so largely by their musical performances.

Resolved, That we are largely indebted to Capt. Brown and the other officers and crew of the steamer *City of New London,* for the pleasure and enjoyment of our trip.

Resolved, That we are under great obligations to Mr. Julius Webb, and other officers of the steamboat company, for their liberal action towards us, and their endeavors to promote the success of the excursion.

Resolved, That we acknowledge the kindness of the officers in command at West Point for the courtesies extended to our party, and the extra military tactics for our special entertainment.

Resolved, That our gratification with our present excursion can be expressed in no better way than by recommending a similar trip for 1870.

Responses followed, and an original song, written by one of the ladies, was sung by Mr. Elkins, to the tune of "John Brown," the whole company joining in the chorus.

We can truly say that this excursion has more than met the expectations of all who have shared in its decided success. We know of nothing that has happened to in the least mar the pleasure and happiness of our party. We have been gone eight days—have traveled over seven hundred miles—had our table furnished the very best the market affords; and the expense has been very small comparatively. We had also quite a fund left which we are to distribute among our party. Our arrival at the station in Worcester was the occasion of some hearty cheering, and

we crossed the old common singing " Home, Sweet Home."
The *Spy* has been hailed with delight, whenever and
wherever we have found it on the route.   w. m.

SONG OF THE EXCURSIONISTS.

We have come from Worcester city, in the famous old Bay
    State;
At least two hundred sixty souls, including small and great;
Our steamer bears us swift along, a gay and goodly freight—
As we go sailing on.
          Glory, glory, &c.

We have seen the crested billows of the foamy, flashing brine;
We have seen the northern river, with its towns and cities fine;
We have seen the glorious Highlands, crowned with cedar and
    with pine,
As we go sailing on.
          Glory, glory, &c.

Some have told us of the beauties of the far-off storied Rhine,
With its castles and its gardens in the country of the vine;
But thy claims, O charming Hudson, we will never more resign,
As we went sailing on.
          Glory, glory, &c.

We have seen the modern Babel, with its countless domes and
    spires;
With its palaces, and hovels where the light of hope expires;
With its missions, and its heathen whose hard lot our pity fires,
As we go sailing on.
          Glory, glory, &c.

Though we've paid relentless Neptune without stint his full
    demand,
We will give to all their honest dues without a sparing hand,
Through rough or smooth, through hot or cold, we've still a
    happy band,
As we go sailing on.

> Glory, glory, &c.

As we hasten on our journey in pursuit of health and rest,
There's a joyous thought unbidden springs in every loyal
    breast;—
We've a broad and glorious country—'tis the one we love the
    best,
As we go sailing on.

> Glory, glory, &c.